A Charlie Brown

Thanksgiving

Charles M. Schulz

SCHOLASTIC INC.
New York Toronto London Auckland Sydney

ISBN 0-590-42437-8

12 11 10 9 8 7 6 5 4 3 2 1   8 9/8 0 1 2 3/9

Printed in the U.S.A.   2 8

What's the matter, Charlie Brown?

I don't know why it is, Sally, but holidays always depress me. Do you realize that Thanksgiving is here again?

Good grief! And I haven't even finished eating my Halloween candy.

What's all the commotion, Charlie Brown?

We've got another holiday to worry about, Linus. It seems Thanksgiving Day is upon us.

Thanksgiving! What do *I* have to be thankful for?

Sally, Thanksgiving is a very important holiday. . . . Ours was the first country in the world to make a national holiday to give thanks. . . . By the way, what are *you* going to do for Thanksgiving, Charlie Brown?

My mother and dad and Sally and I are all going over to my grandmother's for dinner. Holidays certainly do depress me.

Hello?

Hi, Chuck? This is Peppermint Patty.... How have you been, Chuck?

Well . . . I . . .

Listen, Chuck, I really have a treat for you. My dad's been called out of town. He said I could come over to your house and share Thanksgiving dinner with you, Chuck.

Well . . . I . . .

I don't mind inviting myself over because I know you kind of like me, Chuck.

Okay, that's a date. See you soon, you sly devil.

Oh, brother. Peppermint Patty's coming to Thanksgiving dinner. And we won't even be home.

Now who's calling? . . . Hello? . . .

Hi, Chuck. Listen, I have even greater news. Remember that great kid, Marcie? . . . Well, I just talked to her and she kinda would like to see you again, and her folks said it would be okay if she joined us. So you can count on two for dinner, Chuck.

This will be okay with your folks, won't it, Chuck?

Well, the problem is . . .

Don't worry. We won't make any problems. We'll help clean up the dishes and everything.

Just be sure to save me a drum-stick and the neck. . . . Okay, Chuck? See you, Chuck.

How do I always get into these things? Now she's bringing Marcie, too.

It's your own fault because you're so wishy-washy.

Hello?

Hi, Chuck. Guess who just walked in over here. It's Franklin. I told him about the big turkey party you're having and he's sure his folks will let him come. This is going to be the biggest bash of the year! We'll be seein' you, Chuck.

Linus, I think I'm losing control of the whole world. Peppermint Patty has invited herself, Marcie, and Franklin over for Thanksgiving dinner and I'm not even going to be here.

Why don't you just call her back and explain to her?

You can't explain anything to Peppermint Patty because you never get a chance to say anything. I'm doomed! Three guests for dinner and I'm going to be at my grandmother's. Peppermint Patty will hate me for the rest of my life.

Why don't you have *two* dinners? You can cook the first one yourself for your friends, then go to your grandmother's with your family for the second one.

I can't cook a Thanksgiving dinner! All I can make is cold cereal and maybe toast.

Well, we might be able to help you.

Snoopy, you go out to the garage and get a table that we can set up in the backyard. There are going to be seven of us for Thanksgiving dinner.

We haven't got much time, Snoopy. Please get some chairs and set the table.

Okay, Snoopy, that's pretty good. Now come on inside and get the plates and napkins.

Snoopy! How can you serve the food in that ridiculous costume? Why aren't you wearing your chef's hat?

Snoopy! Stop that clowning around and get to work. The guests may be here any minute.

Hi, Chuck. I sure hope we aren't late or anything. We got here as fast as we could.

Say, Chuck, that looks like quite a spread. I bet this is one Thanksgiving dinner we'll never forget.

Aren't we going to say grace, Chuck,
before we are served?

In the year 1621 the Pilgrims held their first Thanksgiving feast.

They invited the great Indian chief Massasoit, who brought ninety of his brave Indians. Governor William Bradford and Captain Miles Standish were honored guests.

Elder William Brewster, who was a minister, said a prayer that went something like this:

"We thank God for our homes and our food and our safety in a new land. We thank God for the opportunity to create a new world for freedom and justice."
Amen.

Amen. . . . Well, shall we dive in, Chuck?

A piece of toast! A pretzel stick? Pop corn! . . . What block-head cooked all this?

What kind of Thanksgiving dinner *is* this? Where's the turkey, Chuck? Where's the mashed potatoes? Where's the cranberry sauce? Where's the pumpkin pie?

Don't you know *anything* about
Thanksgiving dinners, Chuck?

You're kinda rough on Charlie Brown, aren't you, sir?

Rough! Look at this, Marcie! Is this a Thanksgiving Day dinner? Did we come across town just for this? We were sup- posed to get a *real* Thanksgiving dinner.

Now wait a minute, sir. Did *he* invite you here to dinner or did you invite yourself and us too?

I never thought of it like that. Do you think I hurt ol' Chuck's feelings? Golly, why can't I act right outside a baseball game?

Marcie, maybe you can go to ol' Chuck and patch things up for me. Tell him how I *really* feel. Tell him that I didn't mean it like it sounded. You can do it. Tell him I really like him and the dinner is okay with me.

Well, I don't know, sir, I'll try.
But maybe you should go to
Chuck and tell him yourself.

No, Marcie, I'll just ruin everything. I'm too brusque and rough.
You go speak for me.

Don't feel bad, Chuck. Peppermint Patty didn't mean all those things she said. Actually, she really likes you.

I don't feel bad for myself. I just feel bad because I ruined everyone's Thanksgiving.

But Thanksgiving is more than
eating, Chuck. You heard what
Linus was saying out there.

Those early Pilgrims were thankful for what had happened to them, and we should be thankful, too. We should just be thankful for being together. I think that's what they mean by Thanksgiving, Charlie Brown.

See you later, Charles.

Pssst, Marcie. Come here!

Charles? . . .

He's all yours, sir.

Apologies accepted, Chuck?

There's enough misunderstanding in the world already without these stupid misunderstandings, Chuck.

Why, you're holding my hand, you sly dog.

Good grief! It's four o'clock. We're supposed to be at Grandmother's by four-thirty.

I'd better talk to her and explain my dilemma.

Hello, Grandma? This is Chuck — I mean this is Charlie Brown.

We're gonna be a little late. You see, I invited a few friends over and they are still here.

Well, it's just Linus and a girl named Marcie.

And there's another girl — Peppermint Patty. She's a great baseball player. And a boy named Franklin.

No, they haven't eaten. As a matter of fact they've let me know in no uncertain terms!

What? . . .
You mean it?

Peppermint Patty, great news.

What do you know, gang. We're all invited to Charlie Brown's grandmother's for Thanksgiving dinner.

Hooray! Hooray! Hooray! Hooray!